All global publishing rights are held by

Ukiyoto Publishing

Published in 2024

Content Copyright © Ukiyoto

ISBN 9789364949996

All rights reserved.
No part of this publication may be reproduced, transmitted, or stored in a retrieval system, in any form by any means, electronic, mechanical, photocopying, recording or otherwise, without the prior permission of the publisher.

The moral rights of the author have been asserted.

This is a work of fiction. Names, characters, businesses, places, events, locales, and incidents are either the products of the author's imagination or used in a fictitious manner. Any resemblance to actual persons, living or dead, or actual events is purely coincidental.

This book is sold subject to the condition that it shall not by way of trade or otherwise, be lent, resold, hired out or otherwise circulated, without the publisher's prior consent, in any form of binding or cover other than that in which it is published.

www.ukiyoto.com

*"The fire of a woman's rage burns not for destruction,
but for the rebirth of her strength."*

Contents

Feminism Today *By Shruti S Agarwal*	1
Great Escape By Manmohan Sadana	3
Poetry Collection By Rhodesia	12
Her Silent Cry: The World That Turned Away By Dr. Yogesh A Gupta	19
The Bravery of 'Kalika the Mentor' By Aurobindo Ghosh	34
The Divine Protector By Sanjai Banerji	52
The Family By Chinmay Chakravarty	70
We are not weak By Kajari Guha	90
The Unveiling of Kali By Pooja Jha	96
About the Authors	*104*

Feminism Today

By Shruti S Agarwal

As I was walking by the lane at the time of Navratri, the atmosphere was filled with devotional songs and huge pandals were erected in different localities of the town. I came across a beautiful pandal of Durga along with Saraswati and Kali beside her. She was riding on a lion. An extraordinary calm and peacefulness was exuding from her face.

She is the mother of all. She is the saviour of good people and destroyer of bad people. Her endeavour is to bring victory over evil. As I was looking at her with reverence, I heard a conversation between a group of young and old ladies. They were discussing aspects of Durga, Lakshmi, and Annapurna. They were narrating a tale of their maid who washes utensils in their homes. She was uneducated, poor and a mother of two children. Her husband did not support the family due to his bad habits and often beat his wife. But like a mother, she tolerated all ordeals bravely. She deposited the money in a bank, she worked to feed her children and pay their school fees and other necessities of the house. They were talking of her tough life as well as praising her for playing the role of Lakshmi, Saraswati and Annapurna.

2

God has made man and woman equal. But unfortunately, the women are forced to be commanded, disrespected and punished by menfolk. All talks of education and impunity are useless. Though it is surprising that while men worship Goddess yet they forget to love and respect their daughter, wife, sister, and mother.

In Sanskrit it is told God dwells in those houses where the men respect women. I thought Navratri and other festivals are celebrated to make us remember this aspect of human life. Some follow it, some defy it.

Great Escape

By Manmohan Sadana

The date was 15th August 1947, and the monsoon rains had begun their descent upon the subcontinent. But the rains were not enough to wash away the rising tide of hatred that had begun to sweep across the land. India and Pakistan had been declared separate nations, and the partition was tearing apart the very fabric of lives that had been interwoven for centuries.

The streets of Rawalpindi, once a bustling hub of commerce and culture, now echoed with the sounds of fear and uncertainty. Shanti Kaur, a woman in her late forties, stood outside her modest home, her two teenage sons, Jagjit and Onkar, beside her. Their faces were taut with worry as they gazed at the bundles, they had hastily packed. The announcement of the partition had been followed by a surge of violence, and the streets were no longer safe for those who did not belong to the majority.

Shanti Kaur, a mother of two clean shaved Sikh sons, knew that staying in Rawalpindi was no longer an option. They had to leave, and they had to leave now.

"We'll go to Delhi," Shanti Kaur said, her voice steady, despite the fear in her heart. "I have a cousin there. We'll be safe."

Jagjit, the elder of the two brothers, looked at his mother with a mixture of determination and anxiety.

"But Ma, the train stations... they say it's not safe. People are being killed just for being on the wrong side."

Shanti Kaur placed a hand on her son's shoulder, her touch meant to reassure him, though she herself was trembling.

"We have no choice, Jit. We must leave. We'll stay together, and we'll be careful. We'll make it to Delhi."

The journey to the railway station was fraught with tension. Shanti Kaur and her sons moved through the streets with hurried steps, their eyes darting from shadow to shadow, wary of anyone who might recognize them. The air was thick with the smell of burning homes, and the once-familiar neighbourhood now felt like a war zone. When they finally reached the station, the scene was one of utter chaos. Hundreds of people were crammed onto the platforms, desperate to escape the violence that had engulfed the city. The train to Delhi was due to arrive any moment, and the station was a battlefield in itself. Hindu and Sikh families huddled together in one section of the platform, while Muslims gathered on the opposite side; each group eyeing the other with a mix of fear and suspicion.

Shanti Kaur pulled her sons close to her, their small bundle of belongings clutched tightly in her hands. As they waited, a commotion erupted near the ticket counter. A group of men, identifiable as Sikhs by their turbans, were being harassed by a mob of angry young men. Shanti Kaur instinctively pulled her sons back, hoping to avoid drawing attention to themselves.

"Let them go!" one of the Sikh men shouted, holding up his hands in a gesture of peace.

"We are just trying to get to Amritsar!"

But the mob was not interested in peace. Their leader, a wiry man with a scar across his cheek, sneered at the Sikhs.

"This is our land now! Go back where you belong, or face the consequences!"

Shanti Kaur's heart pounded in her chest as she watched the confrontation escalate. She could see the fear in the eyes of the Sikh men, and it mirrored her own. She whispered a silent prayer, hoping that they would be spared the violence. Suddenly, the whistle of the approaching train cut through the air, and the crowd surged forward. Shanti Kaur tightened her grip on her sons' hands and pushed through the throng of bodies, desperate to reach the train before it was too late. The train was already packed with passengers, but they managed to find a small space in one of the carriages. They squeezed in, the metal walls pressing against them as more people piled in behind them.

Inside the carriage, the tension was palpable. People clung to their belongings, their eyes darting nervously around the crowded space. Shanti Kaur could feel the fear in the air, and she knew that everyone was thinking the same thing:

Who among us is a friend, and who is a foe?

An elderly man sitting across from them, dressed in a simple kurta-pajama, leaned forward and spoke in a low voice.

"Where are you headed, sister?"

"Delhi," Shanti Kaur replied cautiously, not wanting to reveal too much.

The man nodded, his eyes scanning the carriage.

"I'm going to stay with my brother in Lucknow. This journey... it's dangerous. But we have no choice, do we?"

"No," Shanti Kaur agreed, her voice barely above a whisper.

"We have no choice."

A young woman sitting beside the old man, her head covered in a veil, spoke up.

"My husband and I are headed to Lahore. We're Muslims, but... we were living in a Hindu neighbourhood. It wasn't safe for us anymore."

There was a brief, uncomfortable silence as the passengers absorbed her words. It was clear that everyone was on edge, wary of revealing too much about their identities. In these times, one's religion could mean the difference between life and death.

Jagjit glanced at the young woman; his curiosity piqued.

"Were you... were you safe there?"

She shook her head, her eyes welling up with tears.

"No. They... they came for us in the night. We were lucky to escape."

Shanti Kaur squeezed Jagjit's hand, silently urging him not to ask any more questions. The last thing they needed was to draw attention to themselves. As the train hurtled through the countryside, the atmosphere inside the carriage grew increasingly tense. The passengers spoke in hushed tones, their conversations punctuated by nervous glances. Shanti Kaur could see the fear in their eyes, and she knew that they were all thinking the same thing:

Would they make it to their destination alive?

At one of the stations, the train came to an abrupt halt. The doors were flung open, and a group of armed men stormed the carriage. They were shouting slogans, their faces twisted with anger.

"What are your names!" one of the men demanded, brandishing a rifle.

The passengers froze, terror etched on their faces. Shanti Kaur felt her heart stop. If they discovered her Sikh identity, there was no telling what they would do. The old man who had spoken to Shanti Kaur earlier was the first to act. He slowly reached into his pocket and pulled out a small booklet.

"I'm just an old man," he said, his voice trembling. "Please, let us go in peace."

The leader of the group snatched the booklet from the old man's hands and glanced at it. It had his name and picture on it. After a tense moment, he handed it back with a grunt. Suddenly, he pulled him from the collar and passed him to his partner, who dragged him away. After a couple of minutes a scream was heard and Shanti Kaur bend towards the corridor to see a blood stained sword.

Shanti Devi watched in horror as the men moved through the carriage, checking their religious identity, their eyes cold and unforgiving. When they reached her, she held her breath, her heart pounding in her chest. The man glanced at her with a knowing and penetrating look. There was a moment of silence, and she could feel the eyes of the other passengers on her. Finally, the man without saying a word moved on. He was Irfan Khan who owned a grocery shop and lived in their lane near Lunda Bazaar in Rawalpindi. Shanti Devi let out a breath of relief. She clutched her sons close, grateful that they had been spared. The rest of the journey passed in tense silence.

The train made several more stops, each time filling the passengers with dread as they waited to see if they would be targeted. But finally, after what felt like an eternity, the train pulled into the station in Delhi. As the train came to a stop, the passengers began to disembark, their relief palpable. Shanti Kaur and her sons stepped onto the platform, the familiar sights and sounds of Delhi a stark contrast to the terror they had just experienced. Shanti Kaur looked around, tears of relief in her eyes. They had made it. They were safe.

"Ma," Onkar said, his voice choked with emotion. "We're home."

Shanti Kaur smiled through her tears and hugged her sons tightly. They had survived the journey, and now they could begin to rebuild their lives. But the scars of the partition would remain with them forever, a reminder of the horrors they had witnessed. As they walked away from the station towards Hailey Road , Shanti Kaur looked back at the train, now empty and silent. She knew that the journey had changed them all, and that the memories of that night would haunt them for the rest of their lives. But they had survived, and for now, that was enough.

As months passed, Shanti Kaur in November sat on a chair in her cousin's house in Hailey Road, New Delhi and sipped hot tea while reading the following dirge written by the famous poet Amrita Pritam,

"Aj aakhan Waris Shah nu ki tun kabran vichchon bol,

Te aj kitab-e-ishq da koi agla varka phol.

Ik roi si dhee Punjab di, tun likh likh maare vain,

Aj lakhan dheean rondian tainu Waris Shah nu kahen.

Uth dardmandaan dia dardiaa, uth takk apnaa Punjab,

Aj bele lashan bichhian te lahu di bhari Chenab"

(Today, I ask Waris Shah to speak from the grave,

and turn the next page in the Book of Love.

Once, one daughter of Punjab cried, you wrote long wailing sagas,

Today, millions of daughters are crying out to you, Waris Shah!

Rise! O empathiser of the victims, rise and look at your Punjab,

Today, the farms are strewn with corpses, and blood fills the Chenab)

Poetry Collection

By Rhodesia

The Beautiful Badass

The femme was born with an angelic face,

Yet her first cry resounded mighty voice,

From her sweet eyes exuded piercing stares,

Particular to patterns of her choice.

When sweet little girls with cute ponytails

Were playing dress-and-make-up pretty dolls,

She was prying on stars and universe,

Amassing knowledge, and solving puzzles.

While teenage lasses waited for the lads,

Day-dreaming of romance and holding hands,

She focussed on her lessons to be learned,

Reaping recognitions her hard work earned.

In all her works, her brilliance bedazzled,

Left her mark whatever task mandated,

Despite her calm and unassuming ways,

She surely makes her turf a better place.

Her marriage had a wondrous wedding feast,

And not too long her womb was blessed with babes,

She savored her domestic life with zest,

Her little home, a warm and spotless nest.

What once hailed her asset was her beauty,

14

Breeded her partner's insecurity,

While she toiled to build her home with safety,

Her husband wrecked with negativity.

It was taboo to her society,

To break the vows and split a family,

Amid accusations, she stood her ground,

Her will was strong to turn her fate around.

Arising from ashes, she built her home,

A lone parent to children of her own,

She feared not, for she had ample income,

To raise her kids in peace and love alone.

Now unfettered from shackles of the past,

She resolved to live life to the fullest,

Leaving in her field legacies that last,

While grooming her kids to their very best.

She, the beautiful badass till the end,

Attracted suitors hoping she would bend,

But she remained a rose of no man's land,

And cherished all her lovers as her friends.

Master of Space and Time

My little boy once asked,

Mamma, why is it that when I play a game

Time runs so fast,

But a boring class

Seems to slow down time?

Who now is powerful enough

To be above

That merciless Tyrant

Who has enslaved both master and servant,

But the consciousness of each one?

Indeed, what is time?

On what is it based?

Is it not an invention of man

To meet his ends,

Only to be its slave in the end?

Is it not that a moment with a lover

Seems to last forever?

Or when immersed in a passion,

Time seems to pass on,

Without perception?

It's high time to understand

The utter might and freedom

Of the Consciousness of Man

Traversing space and time

Under our stern command.

Is it not that when we stare

Upon pristine clouds on an azure sky

Our consciousness is there

Though our body is here,

Then why not always let our minds fly?

Is it not that all our senses

Are to serve our experience

To incorporate in our reminiscence?

Then why not expand our awareness

And let it shatter our defenses?

What then is fantasy

But an augmented reality

And an infinite imagination

Is a universe of its own

Transcending limitations?

Her Silent Cry: The World That Turned Away

By Dr. Yogesh Gupta

Dr. Maya Kapoor had always been a beacon of hope and light. With her sharp intellect and compassionate heart, she quickly became one of the most respected young doctors in the border state of Arunachal Pradesh. She had chosen this remote region for its need for good medical care, unaware that her path would soon darken with the shadows of corruption and greed.

Maya had grown up with stories of Mahakali, the fierce goddess who destroys evil to protect the innocent. These tales from her childhood resonated with her as she entered medical school. Her mother often said, "The world is not just a place of healing; sometimes, you must fight to protect what is right." Maya never thought these words would apply so directly to her life as a doctor.

Chapter 1: The Rising Suspicion

Maya's days at the college hospital were filled with challenges. Her dedication to her patients was unparalleled. However, she began to notice disturbing patterns. Patients from the nearby villages would come in for minor ailments but would often disappear without a trace. In some cases, families were told their loved ones had died, yet the bodies were never returned. Medical supplies frequently went missing, and Maya overheard whispers among the staff about certain patients being sent to "special wards" where no one returned.

Her first clue came when she treated a young man named Ravi, who had been admitted for a minor infection. He was terrified, and Maya noticed that he had fresh surgical scars, though his medical records showed no history of surgery. When she questioned him, Ravi refused to speak, his eyes pleading for help. The next day, he was gone, and the staff claimed he had been discharged, though Maya found no discharge papers.

Maya's growing suspicions led her to start investigating quietly. She began asking subtle questions, reviewing patient records late into the night, and keeping a close eye on the hospital's activities. What she uncovered left her cold. It was not just an organ trafficking ring; it was a well-oiled machine involving hospital staff, corrupt officials, and even some of her fellow doctors.

Chapter 2: The Revelation

The border state was a hotbed for illegal activities due to its proximity to neighboring countries. Drug smuggling, human trafficking, and organ trade were rampant, and the hospital where Maya worked was a central hub in this dark trade. The state authorities were either too corrupt or too scared to intervene. Many who tried to uncover the truth had vanished.

Maya's investigations led her to a secret file hidden deep within the hospital's database. The file contained a list of patients who had "disappeared" after coming to the hospital, along with detailed records of their organs harvested and sold on the black market. The scale of the operation was staggering, and the names of the perpetrators were shocking—people she had trusted and respected.

One name stood out among the rest: Dr. Arun Verma, the head of the hospital and her mentor. Dr. Verma had always been kind and supportive, but the evidence against him was undeniable. The files showed that he was the mastermind behind the organ trafficking ring, using his position to cover up the crimes and silence anyone who got too close to the truth.

Chapter 3: The Transformation

The revelation shook Maya to her core. She realized that she could not fight this battle alone. But she also knew that she could not ignore the horrors she had uncovered. The stories of Mahakali echoed in her mind. If she could not heal the world with her hands, she would protect it with her fury.

Maya began gathering evidence, but she knew that simply going to the authorities would be futile. The corruption was too deep. She needed to expose the truth to the world. She contacted a journalist she trusted, Raghav, who had a reputation for fearlessly exposing corruption. Together, they began planning how to bring down the organ trafficking ring.

But Maya knew that gathering evidence and leaking it to the press was not enough. The criminals had to be stopped before they could cover their tracks or flee. She started assembling a group of trusted colleagues who were equally appalled by what was happening. They trained in secret, preparing to act when the time was right.

Chapter 4: The Wrath of Mahakali

The day of reckoning arrived when a shipment of organs was scheduled to be transported across the border. Maya and her team, armed with the evidence they had gathered, launched their plan. They infiltrated the hospital's underground facility where the organs were being prepared for shipment. With Raghav's help, the local media was alerted, and the story was ready to break at the right moment.

Maya confronted Dr. Verma in his office, her calm exterior barely hiding the storm within. He looked at her with a mix of disdain and amusement.

"You should have stayed out of this, Maya," he said coldly. "You have no idea who you're dealing with."

But Maya was no longer just Dr. Maya Kapoor. She had transformed into a force of nature, driven by the spirits of those who had suffered and died because of Verma's greed. She responded with the calm fury of Mahakali herself.

"I know exactly who I'm dealing with, Dr. Verma," she replied. "And I'm here to end this."

Maya's team moved in, securing the facility and rescuing the patients who were being prepped for organ harvesting. They gathered all the evidence, including video footage, and sent it to Raghav, who was already broadcasting the story to the world. The news exploded, and within hours, the authorities, pressured by the media and public outrage, had no choice but to act.

Dr. Verma and his accomplices were arrested, but not before a tense standoff in which Maya had to use all her medical skills and knowledge of the hospital to outmaneuver them. The raid exposed the full extent of the operation, implicating officials and criminals across the region.

Chapter 5: The Aftermath

The fallout was immense. The government was forced to act, and a massive crackdown on organ trafficking and drug smuggling followed. Hospitals across the region were investigated, leading to the arrest of numerous corrupt officials and medical professionals. The people who had suffered at the hands of this network finally received justice, though nothing could bring back those who had lost their lives.

Maya's actions made her a hero, but she shunned the spotlight. She returned to her work, more dedicated than ever to healing and helping those in need. But the fire within her, the spirit of Mahakali, never left. She knew that the world was full of darkness, and sometimes, the only way to protect the innocent was to fight against the evil with everything she had.

In the years that followed, Maya continued to work as a doctor, but she also became a symbol of resistance against corruption and injustice. Her story inspired many to stand up against wrongdoing, no matter the cost. For Maya, the battle was not over—it never would be. But she was ready for whatever came next, knowing that as long as she had the spirit of Mahakali within her, she could face anything.

And so, Dr. Maya Kapoor, once a healer, now a warrior, continued her journey, determined to bring light into the darkest corners of the world, one step at a time.

This was a reel ending. But in reality this is not the case. Let's see what really happened.

Chapter 5: The Descent into Darkness

Maya's determination to expose the horrific organ trafficking ring had brought her closer to the truth than anyone before. With the help of Raghav, the journalist, and a small group of trusted friends, she had gathered irrefutable evidence. But as they prepared to blow the lid off the operation, their enemies caught wind of their plans.

One evening, after a grueling day at the hospital, Maya was confronted by a group of men in suits—representatives of the powerful network she was trying to bring down. They spoke in cold, measured tones, threatening her with veiled implications. They knew everything about her—where her parents lived, who her friends were, and every detail of her life. The message was clear: if she continued on her path, they would destroy everyone she loved.

Maya's friends were terrified. They knew that these criminals had deep political connections and the backing of corrupt police officers. The risks were too high. One by one, they backed out, begging Maya to do the same. But Maya refused to bow to fear. She had come too far to turn back now. She told them that if they did not stand against this evil, no one would. But in their eyes, she saw only terror and resignation.

Left alone, Maya knew she was in grave danger, but she could not bring herself to abandon the fight. She sent all the evidence to Raghav, asking him to keep it safe and release it if anything happened to her. The night was dark and heavy with an ominous silence as she returned to her small apartment, exhausted but resolute.

Chapter 6: The Assault

In the dead of night, as Maya lay in bed, the darkness descended upon her in the form of brutal violence. A group of ten to twelve men stormed into her apartment, their faces masked but their intentions clear. They dragged her from her bed, and before she could scream for help, they began to torture her.

The assault was savage, relentless. These were men who had long since shed any humanity. They beat her, humiliated her, and violated her in the most horrific ways. But through it all, Maya refused to beg for mercy. She knew that this was her end, but she would not give them the satisfaction of seeing her break.

When they were done, they left her broken body on the floor, a stark warning to anyone who might dare to stand against them. But even in her last moments, Maya clung to the hope that her death would not be in vain.

Chapter 7: The Spark of Revolution

Maya's mutilated body was discovered the next morning, and the news of her murder spread like wildfire. Raghav, true to his promise, released the evidence to the media. The story of Maya Kapoor, the brave doctor who had sacrificed her life to expose a monstrous crime, ignited a wave of outrage across the country.

Doctors everywhere, inspired by Maya's courage and horrified by her fate, began to protest. What started as a local movement quickly grew into a national and then international outcry. Hospitals shut down as doctors walked out in solidarity. The streets filled with white coats as medical professionals from all over the country demanded justice for Maya. The protest grew beyond the medical community, drawing in ordinary citizens who were appalled by the corruption and brutality that had claimed Maya's life.

The pressure became too much for the government to ignore. Reluctantly, they were forced to bring in the Central Bureau of Investigation (CBI) to handle the case.

The CBI, under immense public scrutiny, launched a thorough investigation. The evidence Maya had gathered, combined with the sheer force of the protests, left them no choice but to act.

Chapter 8: Justice for Maya

The investigation revealed the full extent of the criminal network. It was not just doctors and hospital staff; high-ranking politicians, police officials, and influential businessmen were all implicated. The nation watched in disbelief as the powerful men who had seemed untouchable were arrested and brought to trial.

The legal battle was long and arduous, with the accused using every trick in the book to delay and derail the proceedings. But the relentless pressure from the public, led by the medical community, kept the wheels of justice turning. Maya's story had become a symbol of resistance, and the country would not rest until those responsible were held accountable.

Finally, after years of legal wrangling, the verdict was delivered. Every single one of the criminals—those who had directly attacked Maya, those who had orchestrated the organ trafficking ring, and those who had protected the operation with their political power—were found guilty. They were sentenced to life in prison without the possibility of parole.

Chapter 9: The Legacy of a Warrior

Maya Kapoor's death had sparked a revolution. The reforms that followed the case led to a crackdown on corruption in the medical field and stricter regulations to prevent such atrocities from ever happening again. Her name became synonymous with courage and sacrifice, a reminder that even in the face of overwhelming evil, one person's stand can ignite a movement that changes the world.

In her hometown, a statue was erected in her honor, depicting her as a modern-day Mahakali, her face serene but her stance powerful, a guardian of justice. People came from all over to pay their respects, leaving flowers and notes of gratitude at her feet.

Though Maya was gone, her spirit lived on in the countless lives she had touched, in the doctors who continued to fight against corruption, and in the nation that had been awakened by her sacrifice. The story of Dr. Maya Kapoor would be told for generations, a testament to the power of one person's resolve to make the world a better place, no matter the cost.

And so, Maya's legacy was not just of a healer, but of a warrior who, in the end, achieved victory through the lives she inspired, even in death.

Even these ending would be acceptable thinking that at least we people fought for the right thing and got the victory. But in reality world the things that happens is following

Chapter 9: The Agitation

After Maya's tragic death, the medical community erupted in outrage. What began as a local protest in Arunachal Pradesh quickly swelled into the largest agitation the country had ever seen. Doctors across the nation united, shutting down hospitals and flooding the streets in their white coats, demanding justice for their fallen colleague. They refused to be silenced, their voices echoing Maya's relentless spirit.

But their defiance was met with an even darker force. The powerful politicians and corrupt police officers behind the organ trafficking ring were determined to bury the truth. They began by systematically destroying the evidence Maya had painstakingly gathered. Files were erased, records were altered, and the trail of corruption was meticulously covered up. They then planted false evidence to frame an innocent man, trying to close the case quickly and shift the narrative away from their involvement.

When this deception failed, and the public continued to support the doctors' cause, the authorities resorted to more violent tactics. They attacked the protesting doctors with batons, tear gas, and even live ammunition in some cases. Media coverage was censored, and the protests were portrayed as unruly mobs threatening public safety. The government declared the gatherings illegal, arresting key leaders and dispersing crowds with brute force.

The turning point came when a massive crowd of over 7,000 people, driven by fury and despair, stormed the government offices in Arunachal Pradesh where the original evidence had been kept. They broke into the building, hoping to retrieve proof of the conspiracy, but found only ashes—the evidence had been burned, and the truth, once so close, was now lost forever.

Chapter 10: The Suppression

The judiciary, once seen as a beacon of hope, now appeared powerless. With the evidence destroyed and witnesses too terrified to testify, the courts were forced to rely on the fabricated narrative put forward by the authorities. Media outlets, once sympathetic to the doctors' cause, were pressured into silence. The protest coverage was pulled from the airwaves, replaced by stories that painted the doctors as extremists and criminals.

The police, emboldened by the chaos they had sown, intensified their harassment of anyone who still dared to speak out. Witnesses were threatened, beaten, and jailed on trumped-up charges. The false case against the innocent man dragged on in the courts, a grim reminder of the state's willingness to sacrifice anyone to protect its own.

The agitation lost momentum as the years passed. People grew weary of the constant fear and violence. The initial outrage that had united the medical community and their supporters began to dissipate. One by one, the protest leaders were silenced—some by force, others by the crushing weight of despair.

Chapter 11: The Bitter End

In the end, the movement fizzled out, and the world moved on. The politicians and police who had orchestrated the organ trafficking ring and Maya's murder continued to live their lives, unpunished and unrepentant. The false narrative became the accepted truth, and those who had fought for justice were forgotten.

Maya's story, once a symbol of courage and resistance, faded from the public's memory. The statue that had been erected in her honor was quietly removed, deemed too controversial in a country that wanted to forget the painful past.

The judiciary, paralyzed by the destruction of evidence and the manipulation of the legal process, never delivered the justice Maya deserved. The media, once the watchdogs of democracy, turned their backs on the truth, complicit in the cover-up.

Epilogue: The Silent Defeat

Today, the tale of Dr. Maya Kapoor is a somber reminder of the darkness that can prevail when the forces of corruption and greed are allowed to rule unchecked. The world failed its Mahakali, allowing evil to triumph over righteousness. Her death, meant to be a beacon of change, became a story of how easily the voices of the brave can be silenced.

In a world that has forgotten the battles once fought in her name, we are left with the bitter truth: justice is not always served, and sometimes, evil wins because we allow it to. The memory of Maya Kapoor lingers as a haunting question—what might have been if we had not let fear and apathy destroy the light she had ignited?

The Bravery of 'Kalika the Mentor'

By Aurobindo Ghosh

The Making of Kalika

Kalika was born in a small village nestled on the UP-Nepal border, where the lush green hills met the clear blue skies. Her father, Shyam Singh, a retired army jawan, was a farmer known for his strong will and unshakable resolve, traits he passed on to his daughter. In a village where traditional gender roles were rigidly adhered to, Kalika was an anomaly. From a young age, her father decided that she would not be confined to the expectations placed on girls. Instead, she was raised to be as strong, fearless, and independent as any boy. During his training period, as a jawan, he underwent rigorous practice in Judo, Karate and later on Kung-Fu. As he loved Judo and Karate, he perused his practice even after his retirement. He was a much disciplined individual.

Shyam Singh had always wanted a son, but when Kalika was born, he felt no disappointment. He saw in her the potential to be more than just a dutiful daughter. Under his watchful eye, Kalika began her training in judo and karate at the tender age of seven. Her mornings started with rigorous physical exercises, followed by lessons in martial arts. As she grew older, she was taught the art of wielding swords and spears, her skill and precision impressing even the seasoned warriors in the neighboring villages. By the time she reached her teenage years, Kalika had earned a black belt in kung fu, a rare feat for anyone in the region.

But Kalika's upbringing was not without its challenges. The villagers, especially the elders, frowned upon Shyam Singh's unconventional methods of upbringing his daughter. They believed that girls were meant to be soft-spoken and demure, trained in the arts of cooking, cleaning, and other household chores. Kalika's mother, Kamla, often found herself defending their choices to the other women in the village. "A girl's place is in the kitchen," they would say, but Kamla, though silent but undeterred, supported her husband and daughter wholeheartedly.

Kalika, however, was undaunted by the whispers and disapproving glances. Her father had instilled in her a sense of purpose that went beyond the confines of her village. She dreamed of empowering the other girls around her, teaching them to defend themselves from the dangers that lurked in the shadows. Kalika knew that the world outside their village was not always kind, and she wanted to ensure that no girl would ever fall victim to violence or exploitation.

Her efforts, though noble, were met with resistance. When she approached the parents of the girls in her village, offering to teach them the basics of self-defense, she was met with polite refusals or outright disdain. The villagers clung to their outdated beliefs, convinced that a girl's worth lay in her ability to maintain a home, not in her strength or ability to fight. Despite the setbacks, Kalika continued her training, hoping that one day the village would see the value in her work. Little did she know that this very training would soon be put to the ultimate test!

Kalika's New Venture and Achievements

After achieving her black belt in judo and mastering kung fu, Kalika's journey was far from complete. She received accolades from various government organizations especially by the health, cultural, and sports departments and NGO's. Her mission to empower the girls in her village by teaching them self-defense was frequently praised by the media. Also life sketch of her achievements was published in local and regional news papers. She became a known face in the region which impressed the parents of those girls who earlier opposed the idea of allowing their wards to Kalika for rigorous physical activities. Kalika knew that the skills she had acquired could not only protect these girls from harm but also instill in them a sense of confidence and independence that would help them navigate life's challenges. Kalika began by reaching out to the families in her village. She understood the resistance she might face, as many parents still held traditional views about a girl's role in society. But Kalika was relentless. She organized community meetings; with the help of regional government establishments where she demonstrated the techniques she had mastered and explained the importance of self-defense for all girls.

Slowly, the village elders, both men and women began to change their minds. The parents who once dismissed her as an anomaly now saw the value in what she was offering. But the adamant parents did not allow their girls to join Kalika's selfless endeavor. This rigid attitude resulted such that many girls remained vulnerable to outside malicious intentions.

Kalika started with a small group of about ten girls. She held classes in an open field near her home, teaching them the basics of judo, karate, and kung fu. The girls, ranging in age from eight to sixteen, were eager to learn. Kalika's teaching style was patient and encouraging, and her students quickly began to show progress. What started as a small group soon grew as more parents saw the benefits of the training. As the number of students increased, Kalika faced the challenge of scaling her efforts. She began to train a few of the older girls to assist her in teaching the younger ones. These girls became Kalika's perfect disciples, learning not just the techniques but also the philosophy behind martial arts discipline, respect, and the power of self-confidence.

Beyond the Border

Kalika's success in training the village girls did not go unnoticed. She continued to compete in various National and Asian competitions, where her reputation as a fierce and skilled competitor grew. Her achievements in these areas were remarkable; she was consistently placed at the top of her categories, bringing home medals and trophies.

These accolades only fueled her determination to share her knowledge and skills with others. In addition to her physical training, Kalika embraced the power of social media to expand her reach. She created profiles on various platforms, sharing videos of her training sessions, competition highlights, and motivational messages. Kalika quickly gained a following of like-minded individuals who shared her passion for martial arts and empowerment. Through these connections, she was able to network with other martial artists, instructors, and organizations across India and Nepal.

Her growing influence caught the attention of the Nepal Judo and Karate Federation, which invited her to train their female students. This was a significant honor, and Kalika eagerly accepted. She used to travel to Nepal twice a month, where she would conduct intensive training sessions for girls coming from all over the country. Her workshops were well-received, and she was praised for her ability to connect with her students and inspire them to push beyond their limits. Kalika's involvement with the Nepal Judo and Karate Federation didn't stop at training. She was also invited to judge local competitions in Kathmandu, Pokhara, and Lumbini. These events allowed Kalika to see the firsthand talent and potential of Nepalese girls in martial arts. She took great pride in her role as a judge, offering constructive feedback and encouraging the participants to continue honing their skills.

Kalika's efforts to create a network of empowered girls were paying off. The girls in her village were not only becoming proficient in self-defense but also were gaining the confidence to pursue their dreams, much like Kalika herself. Her social media presence helped her stay connected with her students in Nepal and other nearby areas. She frequently exchanged ideas and techniques with them online.

Kalika's journey was a testament to the power of perseverance and the impact one person can have on community. Her dedication to empowering girls through martial arts had transformed not only her village but also touched the lives of many across borders. As she continued to train, compete, and inspire, Kalika knew that her work was far from over. She was building a legacy that would empower future generations of girls to stand strong, fight back and never settle for less than they deserved. She wanted to create a band of skilled trainers who will take over her reign in near future.

A Stranger's Sinister Plan

One sweltering afternoon, a stranger arrived in the village, his presence causing a stir among the locals. He was a slick-talking man, dressed in fine clothes that seemed out of place in the rural setting. He made his way to the head of the village Panchayat, Mahipal Singh, a man known for his greed and willingness to bend the rules for the right price.

The stranger introduced himself as a recruiter from a prestigious departmental store in Kathmandu, offering a lucrative salary to any girl willing to work as a saleswoman. He made sure to mention the benefits, painting a picture of life far removed from the simplicity of village existence. Mahipal Singh, enticed by the bribe offered, quickly set about convincing the parents of three young girls (Who were not trained by Kalika) to send their daughters to Nepal. The promise of financial security for their families was enough to sway their decision, despite their initial hesitation. All the three girls with dreams in their eyes started their journey to an unknown destination with unknown stranger. Even their parents went to the bus stand along with village head to bid farewell to their daughters without knowing their real fate.

Word of this deal reached Kalika through a trusted friend. Her instincts immediately told her that something was amiss. She had heard of similar stories in the past, where girls from remote villages were lured away with promises of good jobs, only to disappear without a trace. Kalika knew she had to act fast. She confronted Mahipal Singh, the village head, demanding to know the name and address of the departmental store. Sensing her determination, he gave her the name of a well-known store in Kathmandu, which was given to him by the stranger; but Kalika was not easily to be fooled. She had her suspicions and decided to reach out to a judo instructor she knew in Nepal, asking him to verify the authenticity of the recruiter's claims.

While she waited for a response, Kalika's anxiety grew. She knew time was of the essence, and she couldn't afford to be wrong. Her worst fears were confirmed when she received word that the said store had never hired a middleman to recruit salesgirls, and that no such opportunity existed. The girls were in grave danger, and Kalika was the only one who could save them. Without wasting a moment, Kalika made a small team of her warrior brothers and sisters, all of whom had trained with her in martial arts. Together, they rushed to the bus stand, hoping to intercept the girls before they could board the bus to Kathmandu. But when they arrived, they found the parents returning, their daughters already on their way to Nepal.

The situation was dire, but Kalika refused to give up. She knew she had to act quickly if she was to rescue the girls before they disappeared into the dark underworld of human trafficking. With steely determination, Kalika and her team set off for Nepal, using every resource at their disposal to track down the bus and the girls.

The journey was fraught with challenges. The traffickers were cunning, using every trick in the book to throw off their pursuers. But Kalika's training had prepared her for this moment. She used her skills to outmaneuver the criminals, gathering information and piecing together clues that would lead her to the girls.

The Investigation takes off: A Race against Time

Kalika's determination to rescue the abducted girls from the clutches of human traffickers intensified after discovering the truth. The girls, sold to three different massage centers in Kathmandu, Lumbini, and Pokhara, were now in grave danger. These establishments, notorious for their illegal activities, were fronts for human trafficking, exploiting vulnerable girls and women. The realization that the girls she could not train, whom she still considered her responsibility, were now in such peril sent a chill down her spine. But it also ignited a fire within her, a resolve to bring them back, no matter at what cost.

The first step in Kalika's investigation was to gather as much information as possible. She got the clue that girls were given the task of massaging at different centers. She knew that time was running fast; the longer the girls remained in these centers, the harder it would be to extract them. Kalika immediately reached out to her network of like-minded individuals, many of whom she had connected with through her martial arts journey. This included fellow martial artists, social activists, and even some former students who had gone on to work in various fields related to law enforcement and social justice.

Kalika's network proved invaluable. Through her connections in Nepal, she was able to identify the specific massage centers where the girls were being held. These establishments were known to operate under the radar, often changing locations and using bribery to keep authorities at bay. Kalika understood that she needed more than just information; she needed the backing of law enforcement to carry out a rescue operation.

Kalika decided to approach the police with the evidence she had gathered. She knew this would be a delicate task; corruption was rampant, and there was no guarantee that the local authorities would be willing or able to help. However, she also knew that she couldn't do this alone. With the help of her network, Kalika managed to get in touch with a few high-ranking officials in the police department who were known for their integrity and commitment to fighting human trafficking.

Kalika's meeting with the police was tense. She presented the information she had gathered, including the names and locations of the massage centers, details about the traffickers, and evidence linking the village head to the trafficking ring. The police officers listened carefully, impressed by the thoroughness of her investigation. However, they were also aware of the risks involved. Raiding these establishments would require careful planning, coordination, and a level of secrecy to avoid tipping off the traffickers.

With the police on board, Kalika began assembling a team of local volunteers to assist in the rescue operation. This group included some of her most trusted students and a few local activists who were passionate about fighting human trafficking. Together, they formulated a plan to infiltrate the massage centers and extract the girls.

The Raid: A Strategic and Coordinated Operation

The simultaneous actions in three different locations were not just a police operation but a comprehensive effort involving trained professionals, dedicated volunteers, and Kalika's own trained students. These young women, who had been trained under Kalika's guidance, were now stepping up to face one of the most challenging missions of their lives.

The planning phase of the operation had been intense. Organizing coordinated actions in multiple cities required precision and attention to detail. The first step was gathering crucial intelligence. Kalika, with the help of her network, identified the specific locations where the girls were being held. These places were under tight control, making the task of infiltration and rescue extremely delicate.

The involvement of Kalika's students added a unique and powerful element to the operation. Their training, combined with their emotional investment, made them invaluable. They were divided into teams, each assigned to one of the locations. These teams were tasked with supporting the police, using their skills to ensure the safety of the rescued girls and to help manage the situation.

As the day of the operation approached, the final plans were laid out. Each location's operation was led by a senior officer who coordinated closely with Kalika and her team. The success of the operation depended on precise timing and flawless communication. The police units were briefed on the details, including the layout of the locations and the potential challenges they might face. Kalika's students were fully integrated into the teams, with clearly defined roles.

When the operation began, the execution was swift and decisive. In the largest of the locations, the police officers faced resistance, but the presence of Kalika's volunteers made a significant difference. Their training allowed them to assist the officers in securing the area efficiently, ensuing that the victims were protected. The opposition quickly realized that escape was not an option.

In all the locations, the simultaneous operation followed a similar pattern. The place was heavily guarded, but the coordinated efforts of the police and Kalika's team led to a successful outcome. Kalika's team provided critical support, using their skills to help manage the situation and ensure that the victims were safe.

The most challenging part of the operation took place in a location known for its complexity. The building was difficult to navigate, but the police, armed with detailed information, managed to secure the area. Kalika's students played a crucial role in helping the officers, using their agility and training to protect the victims.

The success of the operation was a testament to the power of careful planning and the bravery of those involved. Kalika's students, once ordinary village girls, emerged as heroes in their own right. Their involvement was not just about assisting in a complex operation; it was about reclaiming the safety and dignity of their community. The simultaneous actions across multiple locations were a logistical achievement that required not only manpower but also the dedication of those who believed in the mission.

Kalika and her team moved swiftly. They entered the centers after the police had secured the premises, search for the three girls from their village. In Kathmandu, they found the first girl, terrified and confused but unharmed. In Lumbini, the second girl was found in a similarly distressed state. The third girl, however, was not in Pokhara. Panic began to set in as Kalika feared the worst. But the police, acting on a tip from one of the arrested traffickers, discovered that she had been moved to a nearby location just day before the raid. They quickly mobilized a unit to rescue her. Before the poor girl was moved again, police caught the culprit red handed. To their surprise, they found the person who went to their village to lure the parents of the girls.

The relief Kalika felt upon reuniting with all three girls was overwhelming. They were shaken, but safe. The girls' rescue was a success, but the operation had revealed the extent of the trafficking network. Kalika knew that this was just one small battle in a much larger war against human trafficking, but it was a significant victory.

The aftermath of the operation saw the traffickers being brought to justice, thanks in large part to the evidence Kalika had gathered. Kalika's bravery and determination had not only saved three innocent lives but also sent a powerful message about the strength and resilience of those who refuse to be victims. The rescue operation had been a success, but more importantly, it had shown the village and beyond that girls need not be branded as weaker; they also are warriors capable of fighting back and reclaiming their futures.

The village was in shock when they learned of the ordeal their daughters had been through. Mahipal Singh was arrested; his role in the trafficking operation got exposed. The parents, who had once dismissed Kalika's teachings, were now filled with gratitude and regret. They realized that if not for Kalika's bravery and the skills she had learned over the years, their daughters might never have returned. The story is same everywhere. The poor Nepali girls are sent to India through ruthless middlemen. They lure the parents to send their daughters outside Nepal never to return. The nexus is massive and very difficult to dismantle. Insiders in different areas play a vital role in helping the persons with malicious motives. Only if the citizen becomes alert and keep constant vigil, the vicious plans could be undone.

Kalika's actions not only saved the lives of the three girls but also changed the mindset of the entire village. The parents who once opposed her efforts now urged their daughters to learn self-defense, recognizing the importance of being able to protect oneself. Kalika had achieved her goal, but more importantly, she had proven that a girl's strength was not a weakness, but a powerful force that could change the world.

The story of Kalika's bravery spread beyond the village, inspiring other communities to empower their daughters and embrace the idea that girls were capable of far more than they had ever been given credit for. Kalika had not only rescued the girls from the clutches of evil but had also sown the seeds of a revolution that would change the lives of countless others.

A Beautiful and Sustainable End

Kalika's extraordinary journey from a small village on the UP-Nepal border to becoming a national hero reached its pinnacle when the Government of India recognized her unparalleled bravery. In a grand ceremony attended by dignitaries and celebrated personalities, Kalika was bestowed with the prestigious "Bravery Medal" on the occasion of Independence Day. This honor was a testament to her courage, dedication, and the significant impact she had made not only in her village but across the nation.

The recognition did not stop there. Kalika was also selected to represent India at a prominent international forum, where she would share her story, her mission, and her vision for empowering women through self-defense training. This platform allowed her to highlight the importance of equipping women with the skills to protect themselves and to inspire others to follow in her footsteps. Kalika's voice, once limited to her village, now echoed on a global stage, advocating for the safety and empowerment of women everywhere.

The most surprising and heartwarming part of this entire journey was the transformation in the mindset of the villagers. The very parents who had once been resistant to the idea of their daughters learning martial arts were now approaching Kalika with a different request. They wanted her to open a training center, not just for the girls in their village, but for those in nearby villages as well. The event that had unfolded had opened their eyes to the importance of self-defense training for their daughters, and they now saw Kalika as a beacon of hope and change.

Kalika, deeply moved by this shift in attitude, accepted the challenge with open arms. She was determined to create a safe and empowering space for girls to learn, grow, and become strong, both physically and mentally. With the support of the community and the government, Kalika established 'Kalika's Centre for Excellence in Judo and Karate.' The center was more than just a training facility; it became a symbol of resilience, empowerment, and change. Within three years, it grew into a pioneering institution in India, known for its comprehensive self-defense programs designed specifically for girls and young women. The curriculum was rigorous, combining physical training with lessons on mental strength, awareness, and confidence-building. The center was not only training the girls but the boys too.

Kalika's center attracted attention from all over the country. Girls from various states enrolled, eager to learn from a national hero. The center also started hosting workshops, seminars, and competitions, fostering a community of like-minded individuals who were passionate about self-defense and women's empowerment. Kalika's influence extended beyond the boundaries of her village; she became a mentor and a role model for countless young women. The success of the center also brought economic and social benefits to the village. The influx of students and visitors boosted local businesses, and the village, once known only for its agricultural produce, became famous for its center of excellence in martial arts. The village elders, who had once been skeptical, now took pride in the institution that had put their village on the map.

Kalika's journey had come full circle. What began as a personal mission to empower herself had grown into a movement that empowered others. The girls trained at her center not only learned to protect them but also gained the confidence to pursue their dreams, whatever they might be. They became the change-makers in their own communities, spreading the message that women could be both strong and independent.

In the end, Kalika's legacy was not just about the medals or the accolades. It was about the lives she touched and the change she inspired. Her story became a powerful reminder that with determination, courage, and the right support, even the most daunting challenges could be overcome. Kalika's Centre for Excellence in Judo and Karate stood as a beacon of hope, shining brightly for all to see.

Epilogue

Though 'The Bravery of Kalika the Mentor' is a fictional narrative, the author likes to mention at least two such institutions of national repute which grew big from a scratch. First being the Chand Mishraji Physical Education and Training Center of Champanagar, Bhagalpur, Bihar and second one being Hanuman Vyayam Prasarak Mandal at Amravati, Maharashtra. Author has been a witness to see the growth of both the institutes to become a massive organization from a very modest beginning. The author has tried his best to reiterate that having conviction, even a girl can change the mindset of the masses for good. In the present national scenario, where both girl child and young girls are not safe, self protective manifestation for the girls should be the call of the youth of the nation irrespective of the gender.

The Divine Protector

By Sanjai Banerji

Lord Shiva and Goddess Parvati were in a heavenly realm, bathed in a soft, golden light that radiated serenity. Lord Shiva is seated in a calm, meditative pose on a lotus, symbolizing his role as the supreme ascetic. His ash-smeared body reflects his detachment from worldly affairs, and his matted hair is adorned with the crescent moon, signifying his mastery over time and the cosmic cycle. His trident (trishul) stands prominently beside him, symbolizing the three fundamental aspects of existence: creation, preservation, and destruction.

Goddess Parvati, seated gracefully beside him, exudes a compassionate aura. Her expression is one of deep serenity and love, embodying the nurturing and motherly aspects of the divine feminine. She is adorned in elegant, traditional attire, with delicate jewelry that reflects her divine status. Her presence complements Lord Shiva's, creating a harmonious balance of energy – the union of the masculine and feminine, power and grace.

A graceful deer stands nearby, its gentle eyes reflecting the serenity of the surroundings and extruding innocence and a connection to a harmonious existence in this divine realm. A vibrant peacock fanning out its stunning array of colorful feathers adds grandeur and beauty. A serene swan glides gracefully on a celestial water stream that winds through the landscape.

Parvati spoke with a yearning voice, "Hear me, Lord Shiva. I have long desired to descend to Earth, to see our subjects closely, and to understand how they truly live. I wish to spend time with a mortal and learn more intimately about their struggles, joys, and ways of life. Will you grant me this wish?"

Shiva ponders for a moment, his eyes reflecting the vastness of the cosmos. "I see no reason to deny your request," he replies, his voice deep and measured. "But I will grant you a vision of three mortal persons. You may choose among them and spend one month with whom you will observe to understand their trials, tribulations, humility, success, and innermost thoughts."

With a wave of his hand, Shiva conjures the first vision: the life of Ananya, single, wealthy, and the head of one of the largest pharmacy companies in the country, with her father as Chairman. Ananya is a woman of substance who lives by the ticking off the clock. She travels in a chauffeur-driven Rolls-Royce car and has a large workforce in her many manufacturing units scattered across the land.

Despite her many successes, Ananya remains aloof and has few friends. Her spare moments were spent reading to further sharpen her business acumen. She walked for an hour each morning in her private six-acre garden, accompanied by Alsatian dogs and armed guards.

The second vision unfolded, revealing Priyanka, a celebrated fitness icon, former Miss India, supermodel, and social media personality. Priyanka's life was a whirlwind of activity—traveling to exotic places in India and abroad, participating in marathons and events that demanded physical prowess, and maintaining a strict diet to preserve her lean, sculpted physique. Charismatic and extroverted, she was never shy about displaying her wealth, often seen partying in stylish outfits and mingling with the elite.

Finally, Shiva presented the third vision: Maya, a 29-year-old middle-level executive with unremarkable looks, working in the customer complaints department in Varanasi of a modest company manufacturing hearing aids. Each day, Maya listens patiently to the grievances of discontented customers. She owns a scooter and lives with her parents, who frequently nag her to find a better-paying job and get married. Her life was simple and uneventful, marked by evenings with her close friend Ramesh, a dhaba owner at his roadside dhaba, where they drank tea, ate samosas, and discussed their shared struggles.

Shiva turned to Parvati with a gentle smile. "Tell me, my beloved, whom do you choose to understand the depths of humanity?"

Parvati's eyes sparkled with determination as she replied, "Lord Shiva, you may be surprised by my choice. I choose Maya. She needs me more than the others, and I wish to help her improve her life. Please, grant me this journey."

Shiva's eyes twinkled with amusement. "I knew you would choose wisely, dear Parvati. Go on your mission for a month, but do not reveal your true identity till the last moment as Ma Kali."

Parvati bowed in reverence, touching Shiva's feet, and then transformed into a young woman descending to Earth.

Maya stood at the edge of the ghats, the stone steps worn smooth by countless pilgrims before him. The Kashi Vishwanath Temple loomed in the background, its spires reaching toward the heavens, silhouetted against the vibrant evening sky. The temple bells rang out, clear and resonant, mingling with the distant chanting of prayers.

Priests stood on raised platforms, dressed in saffron and gold, their movements a dance of devotion. They held large brass lamps blazing with flames, moving them in graceful arcs, up and down from left to right. The light cast long, flickering shadows on the temple walls and the river's surface, synchronizing as if guided by an unseen hand.

A gust of wind swept across the water, causing the flames to flicker. The aarti reached its crescendo, the drums beat louder, the chants rose, and the bells rang in furious harmony.

Maya's mind was in turmoil. She had lost interest in her life with the daily bickering of dissatisfied customers who thronged her customer grievance cell, a small room with the plaster peeling off the wall, and a descript table. The rusted fan above provided little solace during summer. Her assistant, a bespectacled 22-year-old man, sat with his laptop cross-checking the details of the invoice of furious customers who came to complain about the dismal performance of hearing aids supplied by the company Maya worked in.

Despite her best efforts to assuage her customers, Maya found herself rudely sidelined in the monthly sales meetings. The marketing manager last month admonished Maya in front of the marketing team in Varanasi and told Maya in no uncertain terms that their company produced the best hearing aids in the country, and that if she was having problems in her department with dissatisfied customers, she was free to leave. In the past five years, Maya, an electronics engineer from Banaras Hindu University, had received scanty increments. Her father lamented the company's harsh treatment of his daughter but was helpless in the matter.

Maya's friend Ramesh, who owned a dhaba on one of the jigsaw lanes surrounding the Kashi Vishwanath Temple, was doing lackluster business but had kept his promise to provide unlimited samosas and tea for Maya as long as she lived. Ramesh was a strong pillar of support for Maya and always encouraged her.

Last week was traumatic for Maya. She was called by the marketing manager and informed that the head office at Lucknow was downsizing, and Maya figured on the list. She would be paid all her dues at the end of the month. Maya realized it was the 15th of April, and she had two weeks to look for a job. When all her dues were paid and encashment of LTA, she would just have a lac in her bank account. Jobs were difficult to get by in Varanasi. She would have to search in Lucknow. But that would mean paying a minimum of Rs. 10000 for a single bedroom accommodation. Maya was faced with a cruel decision. She had to decide tonight on the banks of the sacred river Ganga on the lap of Lord Vishwanath.

As the aarti concluded, the priests lowered their lamps, and the crowd released a collective sigh. Maya watched as small clay diyas, each with a flickering wick, were gently placed into the river. They floated away, tiny beacons of light carrying prayers and hope across the dark water.

As the crowd dissipated, an eerie stillness settled over the ghats. Moments ago, the Ganges had been alive with light; now, it lay quiet and dark. Maya stood at the top of the steps, gazing down at the river, the cool air carrying the faint metallic scent of the water mixed with lingering traces of incense.

Maya descends slowly, one step at a time, each step echoing in the empty air. The stone steps are cold under her bare feet, slick with the river's moisture. A thin mist has begun to rise from the Ganges, weaving itself between the pillars along the ghats and curling around the feet of statues that stand guard over the holy waters.

Reaching the last step, Maya hesitates momentarily, feeling the river's pull. She takes a deep breath, the cool night air filling her lungs, and steps forward, drawn by the promise of the holy dip. But just as her foot touches the edge of the water, she hears a voice — clear, urgent, a woman's voice: *"Don't do it!"*

She spins around, startled, scanning the shadows. The ghats are deserted. The flickering flames of the few remaining lamps cast long shadows, but no one is in sight. Her heart races and calls out, "Who's there?" but only her echo answers. She waits a moment longer, the night settling back into its quiet. Perhaps it was just her mind playing tricks, she thinks, the remnants of a crowded evening still lingering in her senses.

Shaking off the unease, she turns back to the river. She steps forward again, more determined this time, feeling the cold water lap at her feet. The Ganges looks calm and inviting, its surface reflecting the faint light of the stars above. She moves deeper, feeling the water rise to her ankles and then her knees. The river seems to whisper to her, a low murmur that she can almost understand.

Then, just as she is about to immerse herself, a warm hand grips her right shoulder with a strength that shocks her. She tries to turn around, but the grip tightens, holding her in place. Panic surges through her veins. The pressure on her shoulder is unmistakable; it feels natural and solid like fingers digging into her skin.

She spins around, desperate to see who is behind her. Her heart pounds in her chest, and she swallows hard, looking around wildly. The night has grown colder, the mist closing in like a shroud. For a moment, she thinks she sees a shadow move in the distance, a fleeting figure of a woman in a white sari disappearing into the dark, but when she blinks, it's gone. She feels a shiver run down her spine. She takes a step back, out of the water, slowly retreating up the steps, her eyes scanning the shadows, searching for a glimpse of the one who saved her.

As she reaches the top of the steps, she hears the voice again, softer this time, almost a whisper, carried by the wind: *"Not tonight."* And then, just like that, the voice fades into the night, leaving her alone on the banks of the Ganges. Maya returns to her home, Disturbed and shivering from her wet sari. After dinner, sleep does not come quickly to Maya, and she wakes up twice in the night when she senses someone watching her in the dark.

The following day, Maya arrives at her office and is greeted by her security guard, who informs her that a new employee has joined to replace her former assistant. As she steps inside, her gaze falls upon a woman in her mid-twenties, wearing a pastel green saree with deep yellow borders. Her striking beauty is enhanced by her sharp, defined features and dusky skin. High cheekbones, a strong jawline, and full lips frame her large, magnetic eyes.

The woman stepped forward, performed a polite namaste, and introduced herself, "I am Ragini Mishra, an MBA in finance from Lucknow University. I worked for two years at an export agency in New Delhi."

Maya shook her hand and showed her to her workspace. "I'm sorry," she said awkwardly. "The office has seen better days. I'll only be here until the end of the month, but I'll teach you everything I've learned over the past five years."

Ragini replied comfortingly, "I'm sorry to hear that, Maya Ma'am. I wish you all the best in your future endeavors."

Impressed by her demeanor, Maya confesses with a downcast gaze, "I might as well be honest with you, Ragini. I've been downsized, given the pink slip. Now I need to figure out what to do next."

Ragini's eyes shone brightly as she responded with an encouraging voice, "I firmly believe that life always gives us three choices: the right one, the wrong one, and the complex one that your heart and mind see together. Though it may be fraught with danger, I feel the complex choice often leads to the most growth. If we share our burdens, even the most complicated decisions can become clear. God gave us life to face challenges, and we must never give up, Ma'am."

Feeling a wave of encouragement, Maya replies, "Thank you, Ragini, for your kind words. Even though you're a stranger, I feel strangely comforted, as if there's still a chance for me to redeem myself."

With her eyes moist, Maya invites Ragini to sit down. She opens the drawer of her desk, pulls out the laptop previously used by her assistant, and hands it over to Ragini. Over the next few hours, Maya carefully explained how the software works for managing complaints and tracking pending issues. Under Maya's watchful eye, Ragini handles fifteen customer complaints that day. By the end of the day, Maya will guide her in updating the system.

As the day ended, Maya invited Ragini for samosas and tea at her friend's dhaba, and she readily agreed. At the dhaba, she introduces Ragini to Ramesh. They sat at a table for three, tucked away in the far corner, offering a clear view of the scrupulously clean eating area and a fantastic scene of the setting sun against the bustling temple town. Ramesh, a man with a deep knowledge of the Upanishads, began to share his insights. Ragini listened intently, captivated. At one point, Ramesh instructed his head cook to prepare some jalebis quickly for Ragini and Maya.

The following day, Maya arrives at the office and finds Ragini typing intently on her laptop. As soon as she sees him, she stands up and greets Maya.

"Good morning, Maya Ma'am. I was working on a proposal last night, and it's ready now. It's about improving the sales of our hearing aids using the data we've collected in our department over the past five years," she explains. "Currently, our hearing aids come with a two-year warranty, but most issues arise during the completion of a year, particularly with the transmitter, which costs Rs. 5000 per unit. Right now, we're outsourcing these transmitters from a company in China. However, if we switch to an indigenous transmitter from Pune, priced at Rs. 3500, we can significantly reduce our repair and replacement costs."

She paused briefly and then continued, "I propose reducing the initial warranty to one year, with an option to extend it for an additional year at a fee of Rs. 3500. This way, any repairs within the first year are fully covered, ensuring value for both the customer and the company. I've also included a comprehensive analysis of data from the past five years, neatly tabulated for clarity and better insight."

Ragini adds, "You should present this proposal at tomorrow's meeting with the Chief Marketing Officer at our Lucknow head office. If he likes it, you could use the opportunity to ask for a transfer to the Lucknow HO after handling your pink slip."

Maya is stunned by Ragini's ingenuity, especially since it's only her second day in the office. She realizes she's crafted this solution with Maya's best interests in mind. Taking a deep breath, she reviews the proposal and makes a few adjustments.

The next day, a Friday, Maya walks into the head office with her proposal. The secretary, a familiar face, smiles at her and says, "You're in luck! The Chief of Marketing has no appointments today and will see you right after the daily meeting, around 10 a.m."

Maya sits in the lounge, reflecting on the uncanny events of the past few days. Surprisingly, she feels calm, her mind strangely free from fear. She waits patiently, ready for the challenge ahead.

At around 10 a.m., the Chief of Marketing, a tall man standing six feet with a rugged build, enters the room and greets her with a smile. "Hi, Maya. Take a seat and tell me what's new in Varanasi."

Without wasting time, Maya, emboldened by renewed confidence, hands over the proposal in a neat folder. The Chief carefully reviews it, his face severe and focused. After about fifteen minutes, he looks up, a thoughtful expression giving way to a smile. "This proposal looks promising," he says. "Fortunately, my entire team is here today. Please wait here; I'll discuss it with my core team in the next-door meeting room. I'll be back soon."

Before leaving for the meeting, the Chief opens a small fridge behind his desk, pulls out a bottle of lemonade, and places it in front of Maya with a bottle opener. "Enjoy," he says with a grin before stepping out.

What feels like an eternity later, the door swings open, and the Chief walks in, looking elated. "I just heard you were handed the pink slip," he says. "All the better for us! We will move you to a new assignment starting Monday, just two days from now. You've been appointed as the Manager of Research and Development. You'll report directly to me and be responsible for all innovative improvement methods and design changes for our hearing aids."

He pauses briefly and continues, "You'll receive furnished accommodation close to the office, along with all the perks of your new position. Your salary has been quite dismal, with minimal increments over the past five years.

We will increase it to nearly three times what you're earning now. You'll also have a team to assist you. Your current assistant at the Varanasi Customer Care office will be moved to your team, and the Customer Care Office will be outsourced to a private party. With your proposal in place, we may not need to focus on customer care as much."

After a brief pause, the Chief asks, "So, are you happy, Maya?"

Feeling a great weight lifted from his shoulders, Maya beams with relief. "Sir, I'm at a loss for words. I'll be ready to join on Monday."

"That's fantastic, Maya," the Chief replies. "I'll inform HR to have your accommodation ready by tomorrow evening so you can move in on Sunday and be all set for Monday." He extends his hand and adds, "Welcome to the head office, Maya."

Maya's eyes well up with emotion as she shakes hands with the Chief.

After a week, Ragini enters Maya's cabin for a critical discussion.

Ragini began, "Ma'am, I've been working on some innovative ideas over the past week. Since our team is responsible for improvements and design changes to our current hearing aids, I reviewed the designs of the top twenty hearing aid manufacturers worldwide. I then made around 120 modifications to adapt these designs to our products. All these innovations are saved on this pen drive, Ma'am." She extended her hand and gave the pen drive to Maya.

Overwhelmed, Maya replies, "Ragini, I don't have the words to express my gratitude. It's because of you that I am sitting in this chair today. I feel it's some kind of divine providence, and you are somehow a part of it."

With a graceful sway of her head that sent her hair tumbling like a river on a dark, starry night, Ragini responded, "Maya Ma'am, you had the courage and vision to take bold steps forward. I was just a catalyst."

Almost a month after Ragini entered Maya's corporate life, the Chief asked her to attend a meeting with the Varanasi marketing office to discuss the new changes in hearing aids. To his surprise, Ragini submitted her resignation letter. Maya immediately called her to her cabin.

Seeing Maya's surprise, Ragini calmly explains, "Maya Ma'am, I have important personal matters that require my attention. You now have a strong team, and you're making great progress. Please accept my resignation." Crestfallen, Maya replies, "Ragini, if you must leave, I won't stop you. However, I earnestly wish to meet you tomorrow at sundown at the banks of the Ganges, just in front of the Kashi Vishwanath Temple. I will be there after I meet with the Varanasi team."

"Sure, Maya Ma'am. I will be there," Ragini replies with a gentle smile.

After the aarti at Varanasi, sitting on the banks of the Ganges, Maya confides his deepest fear to Ragini, who was dressed in a simple red saree, fluttering gently in the wind.

"Ragini, since you are leaving the organization, I want to share a secret that no one knows — not my parents, not even my closest friend, Ramesh. The night before you joined my office, I was about to end my life at this very spot. I was at the lowest point I had ever been. At that moment, something supernatural happened. A woman's voice stopped me. She said, 'Don't do it. Not tonight.' It felt like a divine intervention, like a hand resting on my shoulder, preventing me from taking that final step. The next morning, you entered my life."

Maya prostrated herself before Ragini on the steps leading to the river. "Ragini, you are not an ordinary mortal but a divine being."

For a moment, Ragini remained silent. Then, she slowly raised her head, and for the first time, Maya saw Ragini's eyes — vast, luminous, like deep pools reflecting both the sun and the moon. Ragini smiled, and there was something in that smile — something boundless and unwavering, like the distant roar of an ocean.

Then, the transformation began.

Ragni stood before her, resplendent — no longer the gentle guide but a majestic warrior-goddess. Her many arms stretched wide, each holding a weapon or symbol of power: a trident, a sword, a conch, a discus. Her face was serene yet fierce, framed by a crown of gold that blazed like the sun. Her hair flowed around her like a dark river caught in a storm. Once gentle and kind, her eyes now burned with fierce determination, a fire of love and protection.

The goddess spoke, her voice resonating like a thousand bells in harmony, echoing the cosmos' power. "Maya," she intoned, her words flowing like a river over smooth stones, carrying the weight of ages, "You have walked in darkness seeking light, and now I reveal myself to you."

"Do not fear," she continued, her gaze softening with compassion, her smile tender like a mother's. "I am Ma Kali, the invincible one, the protector of the righteous, and the destroyer of evil. I am the strength within you, the courage in your heart, the light that dispels all shadows."

Tears streamed down Maya's face — not tears of fear but profound, soul-deep recognition. In that moment, she knew that she stood before the Mother of all creation, the warrior and nurturer, the one who holds the universe in balance.

Ma Kali proclaimed, "Maya, help your friends, parents, and those who come to you in need. Do not worry; I will always watch you, and my hand will always rest on your head."

And then, as quickly as it had begun, the light dimmed. The air grew still. Before Maya stood Ragini again, her red sari unadorned, her face serene and knowing. She smiled at Maya gently as if she had never been anything more than a humble guide. With a graceful nod, Ragini turned and walked into the river Ganges.

Maya remained on her knees, her heart swelling with reverence, her soul ignited by the grace of Ma Kali's presence. The vision of the divine Mother, the eternal protector, filled her with an unshakable sense of purpose. She knew that her life had shifted forever.

In the three years that followed, Maya's career soared. Entrusted with leading the Overseas Marketing departments, she found herself jet-setting across Kuala Lumpur, Manila, Riyadh, and Abu Dhabi, promoting their innovative hearing aids. Her once-small world expanded beyond imagination.

Meanwhile, Ramesh's fortunes took an unexpected turn. One fateful evening, just after Maya and her friend Ragini had left his dhabha, Ramesh discovered a bag containing six lakh rupees. In a moment of virtue, he handed it over to the local police. Three years passed, and with no claimant in sight, the police returned the money to Ramesh, citing that it had been found on his premises. Wasting no time, he transformed his modest dhabha into a full-fledged restaurant. He soon expanded his business further, opening a branch in Lucknow. At the grand opening, where Maya and her family were honored guests, Ramesh's father made a heartfelt request—he asked for Maya's hand in marriage for his son.

The following day, Maya sat in her office, interviewing candidates for her department. One woman entered, dressed in a pastel green saree with a deep yellow border. Maya invited her to sit, glancing briefly at her file. The name on the resume caught her attention—Ragini Tripathi, not Ragini Mishra. She raised her eyes to meet Ragini's and felt an uncanny familiarity. As realization washed over her, Maya folded her hands in silent prayer, looking skyward. At that moment, Ma Kali's final words echoed in her mind: "I will always keep watch over you, and my hand will always rest upon your head."

The Family

By Chinmay Chakravarty

He rushed out of the building, panting and in a state of great agitation. He looked around the rectangular front yard of the housing society campus that he'd been working for as a nightwatchman for the last nearly one year. There was no one around at that relatively late hour of 9 o'clock in the night. The light was burning in the tiny sentry post by the side of the wrought iron gate which was closed. Assured, he walked toward his glass-paneled cubicle, entered and sat heavily on the wooden chair. Hands trembling, he took out his mobile phone and selecting the selfie mode in the camera he checked himself. His hair was ruffled, face flushed and the long-sleeved yellowish shirt tucked into his blue jeans was crumpled. He first did his hair and as he was tidying up his shirt and the collar he stiffened: there was a long red scratch mark just below his neckline—toward his left! Immediately, he started adjusting the breast-buttons of the shirt to hide the mark as much as was possible.

At that very moment he heard a faint sound of a car door being shut. He became alert and cautious instantly, exiting the camera and putting the mobile on the small wooden desk before him. Maybe somebody is either parking a car or preparing to start it in the basement of the building, he thought.

He saw a man emerging slowly from the pillars of the basement and recognized him easily, because he always disliked this forty-something guy who for him was over smart—a man of attitudes and that he always wore a stern countenance and did full justice to it by constantly pulling up the small guys like the watchmen, the cleaners and the like. The man was walking toward the entrance, but he stopped as he beheld the sentry post occupied.

"Hey Raju, you dude! Where have you been? I had to open the gate myself, close it myself! What use of you then?" he shouted.

"So what, asshole! Would the earth tumble downward if you have to handle the gate yourself?" he swore to himself silently and said aloud, "sorry sir! I had to attend to a complaint, only for a few minutes! Sorry sir!"

"For complaints the secretary is there, okay? Don't leave your booth during the night for which you're being employed! In a few minutes all hell can break loose!" the man walked sullenly into the building.

Relieved, Raju began to think furiously: what should he do? He's sure that till afternoon tomorrow nothing was going to be found out which gives him some time to buy; but he has to leave the city immediately, he just cannot take the risk; okay, he made sure nobody saw him entering or coming out, but people like him are always under suspicion whenever something untoward takes place; so, he must pack up and leave for his village home, and maybe come back to the city after about six months when things would definitely die down and be forgotten allowing him to look for a job in some other locality, or maybe he'd go to a different city.

Raju knew there was a train leaving around midnight from the station nearest to where he was now, and therefore there was lot of time to make it. Should I go to my room, change clothes and pack a bag? He thought. No! that'd draw attention and there could be questions as well from the neighbors in that public hell! He made the decision.

Raju picked up his mobile and dialed a number. He pressed it close and tight to his right ear.

"Hello, yes?"

"Aveek sir! It's Raju…er…!" he hesitated and fumbled.

"Yes Raju! Any problems? Tell me, I'm at home!"

"Sir…there's a problem…got an urgent call from my daughter…my wife is very sick and needs to be hospitalized! I have to leave immediately sir! Sorry…but…!"

The line went silent for some moments. Then Aveek's voice came in, "Okay, if it's that urgent you can go. I'll call the day-watchman to come back. Luckily his home is very near. For the nights from tomorrow I'll have to fix someone else. Okay, you push off…and let me know after you reach your home." He cut the line.

Raju stood up immediately and checked if everything was in order in the booth. He pocketed the jotter pen lying on the desk and wiped the visitors' registrar clean. Then he exited quietly through the pedestrian gate.

He hit the main city road after walking for a few minutes along the small lane, took the left turn and preferred walking on the concrete pavement. About half a kilometer away he stopped at a dark area, only faintly graced by the street lights on both sides, and looked all around. The traffic was moderate, and on his side of the pavement there were no pedestrians or walkers at that moment. There was a gaping hole in the concrete slab and he could see the black mass of the stagnant sewerage water below. He looked up at the sky—it was dark and gloomy too, one bout of heavy rains would make these holes spill out water all around, creating one more deluge. Luckily, he thought, there should be no heavy showers for at least till midnight.

Raju felt his right-side trousers pocket and cautiously took out a knife, wrapped in his bloody handkerchief. Drawing out the sharp blade he could see the red stains on it beginning to turn blackish. Without wasting another moment he threw it through the hole and heard the welcome sound of it hitting the water and sinking. He then tore the handkerchief to pieces and making a lump threw it too into the water. He took out his mobile and after pondering for a while dialed a number. On being answered he said in a suppressed tone, "Munna! It's me! I'm in an emergency and leaving for home immediately. If somebody, let it be any goddamn guy, calls you up, you pretend total ignorance about me or my whereabouts, right? And for God's sake, never disclose my village or the district or anything. Are you listening?

"Yes! But what happened? Are you in any danger?" asked the voice from the other side.

"I'll tell you as soon as I am safe and sound in my home! ... well, does Aveek sir know your number?"

"No, he knew my old number only, and I changed it long back!"

"Good! In that case no one should bother you at all!" he cut the line.

He switched off the mobile and then opening its back cover he took out the sim card. A bit sadly, he crushed the card between his fingers and threw it into the drain. He put the empty phone back into his pocket and got down from the pavement into the road, looking for an autorickshaw. He was aware all the time of a sense of great anger and frustration building up within him, almost consuming him. He hailed an auto and set off for the railway station.

*

"Hey Rohan! Who are you dialing all the time?"

"My wife, man! She's not answering the phone!"

"Look at the time, *yaar*! She must have gone to bed early for tomorrow's work! Remember, she's having a regular daytime job while most of us always turn up here as night birds! Besides, by the time she's awake we'll all be dead from the party! So, better let her be!"

"Yeah, you're right! I'll take the next call, okay?"

*

Raju got off from the autorickshaw a distance away from the station. Paying the driver off he looked around the busy crowded street that remains like that irrespective of the night hours. Discovering a modest country liquor bar he went in through the soiled curtains and took a small table quietly. He drank several glasses on the trot to calm his nerves, and then spaced it smoking his bidis one after the other. He also ordered some chicken dishes along with steamed rice. The abundant quantities of drinks and food inside him made him a little slothful, apart from restoring him to his usual normal self.

Now he could go over the past episodes with lot of amusement, rather than with regrets and anger. His stint at the housing society was not so bad, he had a good life. Although he disliked most of the male residents the ladies of the flats always trusted him and welcomed him into their homes unhesitatingly. He too tried to help them going out of the way at times, and in the process succeeded in getting a few favors from some of them, apart from almost all his suppers being taken care of by the resident ladies.

However, the animal inside him scoffed at him disdainfully dismissing such favors as innocuous and always prompted him to aim for the big kills. He'd been planning for that in all those months…and he nearly succeeded this night, just a few hours ago! He had to admit that he was attracted to that tall full-bodied lady in a way that he himself found very unusual. So, he kept her in sight constantly. He gathered that she works in a bank while her husband does mostly night duties at a call center which effectively means that she stays alone in the house most of the nights. By a stroke of good fortune he overheard by chance a conversation between them that this particular night her husband will join a birthday bash right after duty and he will be sleeping in the friend's house through most of the day.

My God! How strong she proved to be! I never imagined she was this capable! Raju thought laughing like a hyena and he was in a mood to delve into the further delicious details which, he knows of course, turned quite a bit scary at the end, smoking his bidis contentedly. But a castaway look at his watch told him it was time to go for the train. He settled the bill giving a more-than-usual tip and left the bar.

He walked the distance to the station, bought a general ticket and went to the designated platform. He joined the big crowd at the place where the unreserved coaches were to be positioned. The moment the empty train came to a stop he joined the hustle and jostle, and managed to secure for him a window seat. A window seat has to be normally purchased from the resourceful porters, but tonight Raju achieved it with his might. Efforts not at all wasted this time, he thought ruefully.

He is used to travel this way for years, and he always manages to sleep in that uncomfortable sitting position, not to speak of the din of the overcrowded coach. But this night he was unable to sleep well, it was full of fits and starts, images floating in his head, some jumbo-sized ones growing even bigger and threatening to blast through him. He also hated the fellow passengers scattered around the seats, the floor and the aisle, just everywhere, and their constant munching of the puffed rice and chatting loudly with their even louder companions or over the electronic devices.

He got down in the morning as the train reached a junction, and freshened up in a washroom he managed on the platform. Then he had a hearty breakfast with hot eatables and steaming cups of teas. He felt much better and looked forward to having a good journey. He began to miss his smartphone real bad now.

*

"What's his name?"

"Raju!"

"Raju what?"

"Sorry Mr. Haque! I don't know his surname!"

"How do you mean, Mr. Aveek?" barked ACP Haque angrily. "You employ someone and don't even know his full name… or native address or anything! You're the secretary of this society and you compromise the security of all the residents! Do you know that before employing somebody you have to give all details including photos and IDs to the police for them to verify?"

"Sorry sir!" said Aveek cowering under the blazing stare of the police officer. "Actually ours is a quite old and a reputed housing society. It's been our practice to employ guys, the absolute minimal of staff as you must've observed already, on recommendations and references. And you see, nothing untoward ever happened here in its two decades!"

"Ah, I see! And pardon me! Who is the blessed person to have recommended this Raju to you?"

"Another trustworthy watchman who's served our society for nearly three years. His name is Munna."

ACP Haque bombarded him now, "That's all I presume! Just Munna! No nothing about him, where he's from, what he was doing where before and so on? Okay! You must be having his phone number at least!"

"I have and I called him! But someone else is answering and knows nothing about Munna!"

"Splendid!" Haque stood up and began to pace around the room impatiently. "You say this is an older housing society, but do your residents behave like the older families did? You see, in today's world we have all nuclear families that entertain no concept of having even good neighbors! Families don't know or bother to know about their next-door neighbors, and how would, therefore, they know or bother about what must be happening in the next-door flat? Even if they hear some frightful cries, why would they care? You must be watching or reading somewhere that if a woman is being molested or raped in a public place the passers-by will either look on or record those sorry details in their smartphones or some of them even join in that barbarity?"

Aveek nodded with his head down. Absolute silence prevailed in the room for some time. ACP Haque sat down and resumed, "So then, here is a crime, and we have not a single clue as to who could've committed it! Okay granted, such mother..." he stopped short as he was aware of a few ladies present in the community hall that he was using for the investigations. "Such brutes could be from anywhere—north, south, east, west or even could be a local! Don't you all agree that nowadays even homes are no longer safe for girls and women...!"

Haque was interrupted by the entry of an Inspector and the head of the forensic team on the crime spot.

"Sir, there's evidence of a tough fight put up by the lady and we're almost certain that although there was a brutal sexual attack a rape is ruled out due to the fact that penetration couldn't be achieved and no semen found either." The inspector reported to the ACP.

Haque looked at the forensic guy and asked, "can you determine the approximate time it happened?"

"Possibly between 7 and 11 in the night, sir. There's no murder weapon, but we've discovered very tiny pieces of skin and specks of blood within some of her fingernails." Replied the forensic head.

"Please make all possible efforts to preserve those for DNA sampling. And try to narrow down the time-frame, maybe later in your labs. Thanks." Haque turned to Aveek after they left. "So, Raju asked your permission to leave all of a sudden and you granted it just like that!"

"Sorry again, sir! But how would I imagine, far from knowing, that such a horrible thing's going to happen or has already happened? Further, in his tenure he never asked for such permission or advance money."

"Do you know he is the prime suspect now, after all the facts we've gathered so far: timing of the crime corroborates his hasty departure; he has most certainly fled, because his mobile is also not working; he also knew that the lady's husband Rohan will be away for most part of today and such information cannot be accessed by an outsider, and therefore he knew he would have ample time to make his escape; and we have no way to search for him around. At large, he's even more dangerous now as his basic objective couldn't be achieved. Aveek, please at least tell me where does he live here in the city?"

"In a low-cost housing colony somewhere in this area where he shares a room with somebody he said!" Aveek was ashen now with huge embarrassment.

"Great! You're possibly unaware that there are scores of such low-cost housing complexes nowadays scattered over the metro. And you'd expect us to search the haystack for your precious needle! ... you see, I can really put you in jail for such callous negligence. Who knows if you were somehow connected to a possible nexus for which in fact, I intend to arrest you…"

Worried and frightened very much now, Aveek began to plead even as his associates and other residents looked on.

Haque was thoroughly bemused by the incessant pleadings of the lone man and the near-total indifference of his fellow residents. He stood up and said, "But you have to come with me to the police station. Can I assume safely that you've at least frequently seen Raju and can ably describe his facial highlights? Describe him to our painter at the station so that we can release a photo immediately."

As he stepped out into the front yard he was directly surrounded by the journalists and camera crews waiting outside. It was around seven o' clock in the evening and the late dusk was finally enveloping the metro city.

*

Gauri does know it well why she had to surrender completely to him from the beginning. Her father was a small shopkeeper who had to marry off three daughters—each time in exchange of a sizeable dowry. She being the youngest one and the groom having agreed to a moderate amount her father thought of never letting it go even if it meant he had to live most of his last days in heavy debt that could've been heavier. Gauri understood all this and agreed. Then she discovered something that compelled her to never think of offering any kind of resistance: her groom had married once earlier and the bride died in a suspicious burning incident; and that from some reliable sources in the village she found the chilling story that her groom seemed to have discovered a way of livelihood out of more marriages, more deaths and more and more dowries where his mother was believed to be an accomplice.

So she decided not to give him any further opportunity even though his mother was bedridden with terminal disease by the time she came into the house, and later as her daughter and the son were born things became less scary. As her groom's three brothers left the village for various jobs and making families the cultivable land was further split up, and whatever was left was looked after by her father-in-law and that was hardly enough to cover the house expenses. Circumstances forced her groom, the eldest of the lot, to leave home and look for jobs outside. Her groom's inconsistencies, short temper and rather a loose character never allowed him to stick to particular job for long.

Now, Gauri thought, things are very different: she's joined a developing self-help group and earning regularly which combined with her considerate father-in-law's sales and crops can make her sail through her household needs comfortably; besides, her daughter, past puberty, is growing into a lovely girl and her son to face the high school exam in the next two years; she wants to continue their higher education to see them successful in all spheres of life; and therefore, now she's more and more focused on how to make the influence of her husband be felt less and less by her children and herself too.

A soft knock on the bedside wooden window startled her out of her reverie. She looked at her watch—nearly two o' clock in the night. Who could it be? She waited anxiously. The knocks were repeated—once, twice and then in a series. A hushed-up voice sounded, "Gauri! Are you awake? Open up! It's me!" she immediately recognized Raju's voice. "Come around to the side door! I'm coming!"

Gauri thought she ushered in a wild animal in the dead of the night: his face is flushed, eyes burning in hollowed sockets, body twitching in parts and clothes smelling filth. "What happened? Why have you come so suddenly—no information, no calls?" she demanded.

"Keep your mouth shut, slut! I'll tell you whatever is necessary later." He began to undress.

Noticing the red scratches on his left breast and at places on his back, Gauri became tense, concerned and very scared. She came up close to him while handing over a lungi and a vest, and demanded in a sterner voice, "Tell me what happened! I must know. You never told me in which city you stay and what job you do! Tell me now!"

Raju gave her an almighty push and as she fell sprawling on the bed all the rage, fury and frustration came back to him, overpowering him. The images in his head became stronger and bigger as he forced himself on her.

How she fought him! He was allowed to enter without any fuss as he lied to her that her husband wanted him to keep a watch over her. Closing the door behind him he wanted to make it a friendly affair. But she resisted violently and demanded he leave the house immediately. As he kept on advancing toward her, she looked madly around for any safety measure. He capped her mouth with one hand for he was afraid she was going to scream and began pushing her with the other toward the bedroom. Both eventually fell down on the sofa and he almost pinned her down. Just when he was getting elated at capturing her, she managed to kick him solidly at his lower belly. He recoiled in excruciating pain for a moment, and in that moment, she made a dash for her mobile. But he leapt on her this time, rolling with her on the tiled floor. In the ensuing struggle she started digging her nails into various places of his body and spat on his face through his fingers. Suddenly then she had her right hand behind his head and pulled his hair back with all the force. He slapped her repeatedly with his right hand. And she started biting his left palm. At that point he lost his patience and bursting with a rage he hardly recognized he took out the knife from his pocket and slit her throat.

Standing up and scared at what he'd done, he waited uncertainly. To his amazement she still managed to stand up, her blazing eyes almost devouring him and her right hand clutching her profusely bleeding throat. She tried very hard to scream, but in vain. Assured that she couldn't possibly scream, he closed the knife and put it in the pocket. Making sure there was nothing that might implicate him he left the house as the automatic swing door closed behind him. He found the passage empty and as he started climbing down the stairs, he heard a click of a door opening. He froze halfway down the first flight of stairs.

The next moment he was paralyzed with amazement and fear. Still clutching her throat she came out in the passage, trying to approach the other flats. But her strength failed her ultimately and she just managed to enter her house, while the swing door shut again. He fearfully climbed up and instantly saw a few drops of blood on the passage floor. He took out his handkerchief and wiped the blood as cleanly as possible. And then he ran down the stairs.

Bitch! he mumbled ferociously, about to finish with her. Gauri, pinned down mercilessly, never experienced such brutality in all the years of their conjugal life, despite his known ferocity. Yet she decided to not run out of the room, for she wanted to know more about what he'd done in the city. Raju rolled over to the other side and told her, "Don't dare making any fuss about me here, right? I'll lie quietly here for a few days. Don't dare announcing it to the villagers. It's strictly within the family, understood? I have some money, so no worries."

"What have you done, you monster?" she cried out through her tears.

"Go to sleep, bitch!"

*

Raju stayed in the bedroom for whole of the next day except for attending the calls of nature, those also covertly. His daughter and son peeped in now and then and he managed to welcome them with smiles each time, but hardly any words spoken between them. That day being a holiday, Gauri kept her children mostly in the company of their granddad whom she's told about his son's homecoming, but no details and her father-in-law didn't demand any. She supplied all the food to Raju in the room—from breakfast onward to the supper and the occasional teas.

By early evening her daughter called her aside and her son also joined in a cluster. They were engrossed over a smartphone—the one she somehow managed to present to her junior college-going daughter. After the absorbing huddle Gauri went out to the cowshed and kept on dialing the smartphone repeatedly, till finally she spoke with someone for a long while. She then held a consultation with her father-in-law which was hushed and extremely tense. However, there was an agreement in the end.

Supper was served in the room for Raju. After completing all kitchen and household work Gauri thought there couldn't be any solid reason for her to not sleep still in the bedroom. She decided she was no longer afraid.

*

Raju woke up late the next morning. Not finding Gauri by the side he instantly got up and locked the door. He found it better to keep the door locked lest some unscrupulous curious relatives barged in.

Presently the door was tried; as it didn't yield there followed a soft knock. Thinking that it must be Gauri with the morning tea, Raju opened the door. It was indeed Gauri! Raju gave her a cracked smile.

Gauri came in and stepped aside, leaving the door wide open. In came two policemen, the Inspector in charge of the nearest police station and an accompanying constable. Without any preamble of any sort they jumped into action—handcuffing Raju and starting to pull him away.

"Hey! What the hell happening here? What the shit you think you're doing?" Raju started shouting hoarsely, terribly scared and unbelieving.

"We're arresting you for the crime you committed in the metro city. A team is coming from the city who'll take you back."

"But what … how … what proof you have? I've done nothing there or anywhere! You can't take me…my family is here…and I'm responsible for their wellbeing."

"They have your blood and skin samples, you swine! You've brought such a bad name to the village!" the inspector clutched Raju's arms to pull him through.

"But damn it! How is it possible?" suddenly he looked at Gauri whose recent actions did confound him. "Is this you, double-crossing bitch?"

Gauri advanced toward them with a stern and composed face. "Take him away sir! Please make sure he never returns. I have to protect my daughter and make my son a good man in future! Take him away!"

"The bitch is lying! She wants to inherit my money and property!" he shrieked. "I have my children! I've fathered them and I take responsibility for their future. You cannot take me away!"

At that moment his daughter and son entered. Raju extended a caressing hand toward his daughter. His daughter pushed it away as his kid brother joined her, holding her hand. And then Gauri came and stood shielding her children completely.

"All devilish traitors! Take me to my father! He'll never disown me. He knows me!"

His father was sitting stooped in an aging chair in the courtyard. As the party emerged from the house Raju ran to him, falling at his feet.

"Oh my dear dad! Please save me from the demons!"

Dad looked at him weakly. "Sorry, sonny dear! I have not the money or the power to influence people in high positions without whose help nothing can be done! Face your fate, son! Some little money I do have, but! I've spoken to the dear inspector here. He'll soon arrange a martial arts camp in our village for our daughters...to teach them techniques of self-defense against marauders like you, son! And yes, I'll spend my little money serving refreshments to the children during the camp days. Inspector, take him away!"

At the bamboo gate the party was accosted by a few journalists. The Inspector spoke.

"Don't interview me! Interview the lady of the house—the family that has just set an example, a very brave one at that! And do remember, don't ever reveal her name or the names or photos of any of the members of her family, anywhere—print, camera, radio or of course, the social media! Right?"

***

We are not weak

By Kajari Guha

We are not so weak

As to be torn up with your beak

The vultures might be there

With a taste of fleshy flare

The hyenas might attack

To dishevel the tidy stack

Of sturdy boxes wrapped

And kept with care to be tapped

In Elegant wrappers divine

Delicate and quite bovine.

Those who enjoy their glory

Of being strong and gory

Let them know the truth

We can kill the brutes

Let us tell you this

We can bring the peace

We can bloom like flower

We can create a bower

If it comes to strength

We can demolish at length

The devilish doom of desire

The monster in human attire

The ruthless criminal cases

With vested selfish bases

We are not the pulpy stuffs

To nurture the ugly duffs

We can challenge like Rudrani

The goddess, who was Kali

The terrific, crimson and purple

Scintillating, gleaming in a circle

Flickering with seven tongues of fire

Headless bodies adorning the pyre

The garland of slaughtered bloody heads

She wears around her graceful neck

The dazzling sword held in her robust hand

Evading evil like the caucus band

Creating Havoc as a tasteful treat

Until Lord Shiva lay at her feet

She halted, felt she shouldn't cross the limit

But the protest must not be timid.

Strong and weak are the eternal poles

The tiger and the lamb,both play their roles.

Markandeya was cornucopia of knowledge

Lord Shiva's devotee ,free from bondage

Mahakaal rescued him from pain

Markandya's devotion was not a bane.

Bhadrakali stepped to protect mankind

From destruction and evil, one of its kind !

We are the legacy of Kali divine

If we wish ,the evils would decline.

Women we are with full moonlight

To soothe and embrace the

scorching summer night

When in doubt or in confusion

We dispel them through liberation

When the roses bloom, the stars shine

The fragrance of Jasmine make you pine

For the healing balm that left you oozing

The bruise of inhuman deeds, infusing

The wounded heart that bleeds for love

We can bring you the bliss with dove

But if the demons try to ping

Our flesh and soul they hit to sing

The minstrel of shame,it isn't valour.

It's heinous crime of human error .

Might cannot be right at all !Never!

When they set the ball rolling forever!

When the hound howls for selfish ends

When power is pelf and lust reigns

When greedy self is in pursuit of desire

Intertwineing the darker recesses of power

Leading to acts of toxic combination

And groping ways to speedy manipulation

The demon seeks refuge in oppression

Permeating anger to bring a revolution.

We offer you velvety solutions

Protecting humanity in the garb of seclusion .

Hark!This is the time to learn

The mother who gave birth to the son

And the daughter or the sister

in the assembly line of mother to be born

Would not linger for justice defied

Goddess Kali is she ! For justice denied !

The Unveiling of Kali

By Pooja Jha

I. Awakening

Raise the girl to be Kali within

A goddess fierce, with strength to begin

Teach her to roar, like thunder in the sky

To shatter chains, and let her spirit fly

Instill in her the fire of self-respect

A flame that burns, and never neglects

Help her find her voice, her inner might

To speak truth, and shine with radiant light

Guide her to wield her sword of wisdom

To cut through doubt, and vanquish whim

Empower her to dance, like Kali's wild stride

Unbridled, untamed, with heart full of pride

II. Empowerment

Raise her to question, to challenge norms

To shatter glass ceilings, and all forms

Of oppression, of injustice, of fear

And teach her to face them, year by year

With courage, compassion, and love

Raise her to lead, sent from above

To break the mold, to forge a new path

And show the world, a brighter math

Inspired by Nirbhaya's courage and might

And the millions who rose, to demand what's right

Inspired by Savitribai Phule's pioneering stride

And the women who broke free, from societal tide

III. Protection

Raise the boy to protect the Kali in front

To unleash her power, to let her ascend

Teach him to respect, to honor and adore

The goddess within, forever more

Instill in him the values of equality

To see the divine, in every humanity

Guide him to wield his sword of justice

To protect the innocent, with courage and trust

Empower him to be a warrior true

To defend the vulnerable, through and through

With every step, with every breath

Remind him of his duty, to protect and respect

IV. Inspiration

From Kolkata's streets to Delhi's gates

The cry for freedom, echoes and waits

For a world where women can walk alone

Without fear, without shame, without being overthrown

From rural villages to urban skies

The struggle for justice, never dies

From grassroots movements to global cries

The call for equality, never subsides

V. Revolution

Raise the girl to be Kali within

And raise the boy to protect her from the front

Together they'll rise, like sunrise high

And bring a new dawn, to India's sky

With every step, with every voice

We'll shatter the silence, and make some noise

For freedom, for justice, for equality too

We'll rise, as one, and see this through

VI. Unity

United we stand, against patriarchy's might

United we rise, for a brighter light

With Kali's strength, and gentle grace

We'll create a world, where love takes space

VII. Conclusion

Rise, Kali, rise, and claim your right

To freedom, equality, and endless light

Let your inner Kali shine so bright

A beacon of hope, in darkest night

With every word, with every deed

Remind her of her inner creed

I am Kali, I am strong

I am fearless, all day long

Raise the girl to be Kali within

And watch her transform, and rise to win

For when she rises, we all rise

In a world where equality survives

Let her spirit soar, let her heart shine

A radiant goddess, divine and fine

With Kali's strength, and gentle grace

She'll change the world, and leave her mark in place.

Additional Sections

VIII. Future Generations

Raise the children to be leaders true

To carry the torch, of equality anew

Teach them to respect, to honor and adore

The goddess within, forever more

IX. Global Solidarity

From India's heart to the world outside

The cry for justice, will not subside

From Africa's plains to America's skies

The struggle for equality, never dies

X. Eternal Flame

Mahakaal

The flame of Kali, burns bright and true

A beacon of hope, for me and you

Guiding us forward, through darkest night

To a world where love, shines with all it's might.

About the Authors

Shruti S Agarwal is a Junior Research Fellow at Symbiosis International University, Pune and is pursuing her PhD in Media & Communications. She has worked with many prestigious organisations like Hindustan Times, Accenture, JP Morgan Chase & Co and more. Shruti is a published author and has two books to her name by the name of Bikhre Khayal and Ek Lamha. She has also been awarded 50 under 50 aspiring authors & researchers by Fox Story India and best contributor in an anthology by Ukiyoto Publishing.

Manmohan Sadana, a retired Joint Director General (Tourism) Government of India is an author, editor, actor and a mandolinist, whose novel – "Healing Strings" has won various awards which include the "Literary Titan Gold Award", "Golden Book Award", "Ukiyoto Emerging Author Award", "Certificate of Appreciation from Kerala Tourism Mart Society" and "Ukiyoto Book of the Decade Award". He has written many short stories which have been published in different anthologies and books. After superannuation from Government Service, he was a student of Persian for three years in St. Stephen's College, New Delhi and presently he is brushing his theatre skills as a student of renowned Director, Activist and Playwright, Mr. Arvind Gaur, in Triveni Kala Sangam, New Delhi.

Kajari Guha is a published author. She is a poet, writer, translator and composer. She has a great command over English, Hindi and Bengali language. She has been writing short stories for Ukiyoto Publication for a long period. Her own books "Euphoric Vendetta-a thriller" and "Pink Rick and Pip.... the Scuba Divers" have made a mark in the literary world. She translated "Tulsi Ramayan-1008pankti mein" from Hindi to Bengali that was published by Ramcharitmanas bhawan, Houseton, TX, USA. She believes in the power of Nature and throws light on the complexities of human mind.

Rhodesia is a multifaceted individual—a Filipina physician, past professor of Medical Biochemistry, past clinical and academic administrator, author, painter, and poet. At the remarkable age of nine, she was celebrated as the Philippines' Youngest Author for compiling an anthology of poems. While presently dedicated to being a loving mother of two, she continues to contribute to the well-being of others through teleconsultations, all the while reigniting her passion for the written word. Her book "Nature and Child's Life Experiences" was awarded Children's Book of the Year at the Suenos by Ukiyoto International Book Awards at Bologna International Children's Book Fair 2024. Likewise, through her book "Soulful," she was awarded Poet of the Year 2024 by Ukiyoto Literary Awards, to be given at the Kolkata International Literary Carnival 2025. She has published a total of 36 books, audiobooks and translations in less than two years since she joined the Ukiyoto Publishing Company.

Dr. Yogesh Gupta is a distinguished senior physician based in Ahmedabad, India, with a remarkable career that extends beyond medicine into the realm of literature. He has authored three books and numerous short stories, contributing significantly to various series. His expertise is further demonstrated by over 200 health articles written for both local and international web portals. Dr. Gupta is also a prominent voice in media, having participated in more than 300 live TV debates. His book, *COVID Diaries: We vs Virus*, earned him the Emerging Author of the Year award. He has a passion for writing on topics that impact our daily lives.

Aurobindo Ghosh a versatile personality After completing B.Sc, M.Sc, M.Phil, Ph.D in Statistics and Ph.D in Economics, Dr. Aurobindo Ghosh taught both under graduate and post graduate students of statistics in Government of Maharashtra College for almost 35 years. After retirement, he joined various Management Institutions as Principal across India. His first poetry book "Lily on the northern sky" was published by Notion Press bagged the award from Ukiyoto Publishing, and subsequently translated in French, German, Spanish and Arabic languages. He is a regular contributor of Ukiyoto publisher's anthologies. Side by side he also engaged himself in creating acrylic, Warli and Madhubani paintings. Dr Aurobindo Ghosh writes poems, short stories in different languages specifically in English, Bengali, Hindi, Gujarati and Marathi. His other literary creations are Insight Outsight; a collection of short stories in English, Mejoder golpo, a collection of short stories in Bengali and Chhondo Hole Mondo Ki; a collection of poems in Bengali. His latest solo award winning book, "Bimladadi's dream" is published by Ukiyoto Publishing. This book is translated in Italian, Turkish and Nepali.

Chinmay Chakravarty is a professional specialized in the creative field with over four decades of experience in creative writing, journalistic writing of news stories and editing, media co-ordination, film script writing, film dubbing, film & video making, management of international film festivals and editing of books & journals. Chinmay had a career in the media sector of the Govt of India during 1983-2019 and after that he has been working as a freelance writer-author. He has so far fifteen books/ebooks published by Notion Press, Ukiyoto Publishing and Amazon Kindle.

Sanjai Banerji is an ultra-marathoner, certified mountaineer and author of four books, Crossing the Finish Line (Running), The Mountaineering Handbook (Mountaineering), Nobody Dies Tonight (Fitness in the Covid-19 Pandemic), a novel Justice on the Hills (Based on a fictional account of Gorkhaland) in five languages- English, Nepali, German, French and Filipino and several short stories published in anthologies. He has a B.Sc (Zoology) and MBA (Production) and is a gold medalist in journalism with 36 years of corporate experience in the steel, paper, and cement sectors. He recently became at 64 the oldest Indian to summit Mount Kilimanjaro with four medical conditions.

Pooja has been working as a freelance writer from past 7 years and worked with several other media houses simultaneously. She is currently writing books and travelling places. She has worked with some prominent media houses like Doordarshan and India Today.

www.ingramcontent.com/pod-product-compliance
Lightning Source LLC
LaVergne TN
LVHW041531070526
838199LV00046B/1618